SAIL AWAY, LITTLE BOAT

To Kathy, Diane, Andrea, Muriel, Barbara, Courtney, Mary Jo, Sally, Jenny, and Jane, the members of my children's writers group who told me this book **could** happen, and to my excellent editor, Ellen Stein, who made sure it did   —J.B.

For Cosmo and Misha   —J.I.

SAIL AWAY, LITTLE BOAT

by Janet Buell

illustrations by Jui Ishida

Carolrhoda Books, Inc./Minneapolis

Let's launch our boat
in the wild roving brook
and watch as it slides and swirls
through the nooks

of a root-tangled bank
where deer come to eat
the tasty green moss
growing thick at their feet.

Sail away, Little Boat,
to search for new friends.
Just follow the brook
till it reaches its end.

Past whirligig beetles
twirling fast on a pool.

Past silver-swift minnows
that scatter and school.

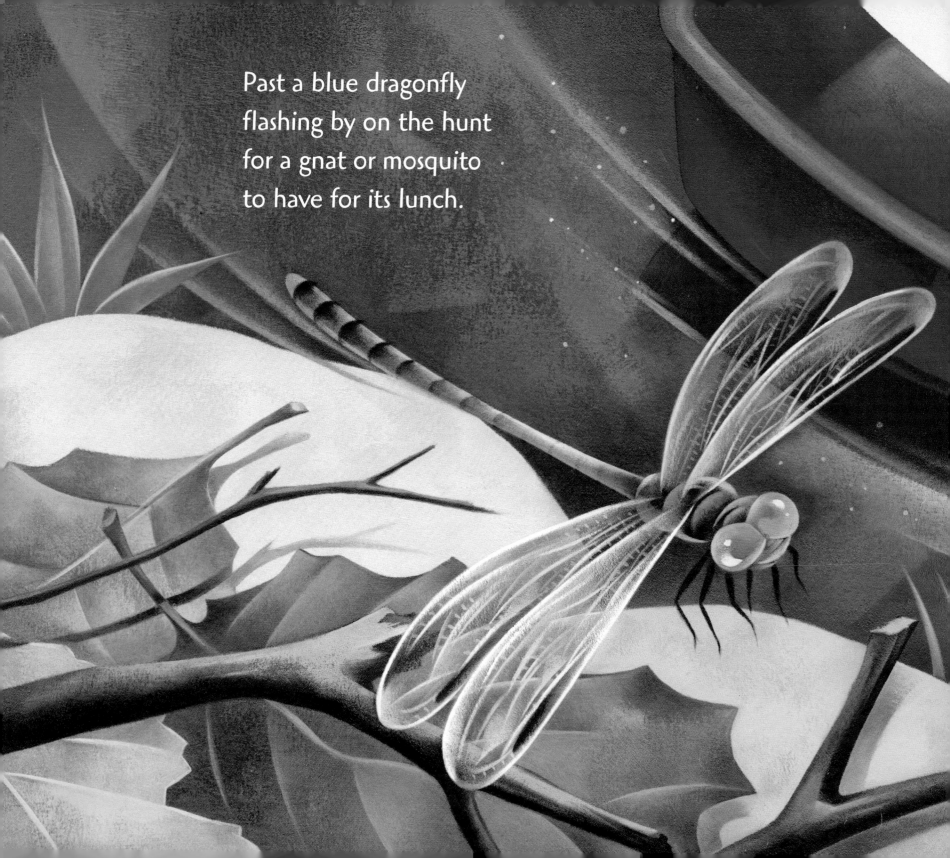

Past a blue dragonfly
flashing by on the hunt
for a gnat or mosquito
to have for its lunch.

Sail away, Little Boat,
to search for new friends.
Just follow the brook
till it reaches its end.

Past a nimble-quick newt
in search of an ant.

Past a prowling red fox
and a trout lily plant.

Past the mink scrambling by
where the giant oak fell,
as the brook tumbles on
with a white-water yell.

Past the slicky-back otter
and his slippery friends
who rollick and roll
through the brook as it bends

over smooth rocks and cool rocks,
a wild water ride,
as lickety-split
the sleek otters slide.

Sail away, Little Boat,
to search for new friends.
You followed the brook and
have now reached its end.

You've arrived where the river
rolls wide, green, and blue.
Sail on, Little Boat,
past a wooden canoe.

Past a fuzzy black cub
and a furry black bear
that snuffle and snort
in the breezy spring air.

Sail away, Little Boat,
to search for new friends.
Just glide down the river
till it reaches its end.

Past a long-legged heron
that pokes with its beak.

Past sun-speckled fish
flashing by at its feet.

Past the bullfrogs that
hide in a thick cattail forest
and croak out the notes
of their splish-splashy chorus.

Sail away, Little Boat,
to search for new friends.
You followed the river and
have now reached its end.

Here the ocean is rolling
and seagulls fly high.
Here big boats and small boats
go motoring by.

Sail on, Little Boat,
where the sea meets the land
under brilliant blue sky
toward the sparkling white sand.

Near the children who play
at the cool oceanside
and love little boats
that go traveling by.

Come home, Little Boat,
you've found some new friends.
Your long, daring journey
has come to an end.

Carolrhoda Books, Inc.
A division of Lerner Publishing Group
241 First Avenue North
Minneapolis, MN 55401 U.S.A.

Website address: www.lernerbooks.com

JUN 19 2006

Library of Congress Cataloging-in-Publication Data

Buell, Janet.
    Sail away, Little Boat / by Janet Buell ; illustrations by Jui Ishida.
        p.   cm.
    Summary: A toy sailboat encounters a variety of animals as it
journeys down a brook, to the river, and finally to the ocean.
    ISBN-13: 978-1-57505-821-4 (lib. bdg. : alk. paper)
    ISBN-10: 1-57505-821-9 (lib. bdg. : alk. paper)
    [1. Boats and boating—Fiction. 2. Sailboats—Fiction. 3. Toys—
Fiction. 4. Stories in rhyme.] I. Ishida, Jui, ill. II. Title.
PZ8.3.B8838Sai 2006
[E]—dc22   2005015003

Manufactured in the United States of America
1 2 3 4 5 6 – JR – 11 10 09 08 07 06